The Courtship of Medicine Paint

By

Genny Cothern

&

Other American Indian Historical Short Stories

PK&J Publishing

1 Lakeview Trail

Danbury, CT 06811

The Courtship of Medicine Paint

Copyright © 2023

Print ISBN: 979 8 86390 6 867

Cover by Darlene Dixon

    This is a work of fiction inspired by three different stories from the long ago past.

    This book is a work of fiction. The names, characters, places, and incidents are products of the writer's imagination or have been used fictitiously and are not to be construed as real. Any resemblance to persons, living or dead, actual events, locale or organizations is entirely coincidental.

    All Rights Are Reserved. No part of this book may be used or reproduced in any manner whatsoever without written permission, except in the case of brief quotations embodied in critical articles and reviews.

    For avoidance of doubt, the Author reserves the rights to this work and does not grant to any person any rights to reproduce and/or otherwise use the work in any manner for the purposes of training artificial intelligence technology to generate text, including without limitation, technologies that are capable of generating works in the same style or genre as this work.

Artificial Intelligence in any form was *not* used in the writing of this work.

DEDICATION

For my sister on the Blackfeet Reservation, Patricia Running Crane Devereaux

And, to my husband, whom I love with every bit of my heart.

Table of Contents

The Courtship of Medicine Paint   page 6

Red Hawk and the Mermaid   page 19

Moon Wolf and Miss Alice   page 39

About the Author   page 70

The Courtship of Medicine Paint

Indian Territory

The Southern Blackfoot Pikuni Tribe

1810

Medicine Paint shook his head as yet another luckless suitor for the hand of Runs-with-elk-woman paced dejectedly away from the lodge of her father, Makes Afraid. What was this now? Seven suitors all turned away in the space of only three moons?

Runs-with-elk-woman, or Elk Woman, was well known to prefer the more masculine chore of hunting over a woman's work of tanning hides and making a home for her future husband and their children. But, though her competence in the hunt was well known, her beauty and her happy spirit kept the young men of the Pikuni Nation enchanted with her. And, ever hopeful, these men (some of the most honored in their tribe) dressed themselves in their best and made their bids for her hand.

But, though she never mocked these suitors, and though she turned them away graciously, it was yet a blow to the men's pride to be sent away.

Medicine Paint had known her since the day she had been born, eighteen snows ago. He had been six winters old then, but he remembered it well, since his father and hers were partners in the hunt; this alone had allowed Medicine Paint to be often invited into Makes Afraid's lodge. He remembered seeing Elk Woman as a baby, recalled again reaching out his finger toward her tiny hand and recollected her strong grip upon his finger. And, looking down at her then, with her tiny head sprinkled with black hair, she had gazed up at him with her big dark eyes and had smiled at him.

Unfortunately for him, the incident, innocent though it had been, had forged a bond between them, even then. It was "unfortunate" because she had gone on to become one of the best hunters in the Pikuni village, even besting him. She had even won foot races, beating both him and the other boys. And she, six winters younger than he!

Always she laughed about it, and, though she never ridiculed him for his losses against her, he yet resented her prowess.

He recalled the day when her father had brought her along to be part of their morning hunt. She had been eight winters old then, and he fourteen, and in his young man's consideration, he was a fully grown man with manly duties. Wasn't he already a well-respected hunter?

"Why is she here?" Medicine Paint had asked his father. Hadn't he, his father and hers formed a threesome?

Indeed, Medicine Paint resented her presence here; he did not wish another person to be added to their successful hunts, and this was particularly so with her because she was a girl. Wouldn't the other boys mock him and ask him if he preferred dresses to breechcloth and leggings?

"Son, do not speak so loudly against her. Know you that her father has failed to produce a son. Know you, also, that he has long trained her to the hunt. And, despite her young age, her accuracy in bringing down game has been often commented upon by the elders in our tribe. Consider, too, how much meat it takes to feed a family of five sisters. She will be a great help to her father in this endeavor. Given time, it is my hope you will allow her to become your partner."

"But, Father, a girl?"

Medicine Paint's father had laid his hands on his son's shoulders, and, bending down (because Medicine Paint had yet to attain his full height), had said, "Do this for me, my son. Her father, my friend, needs her help, and she has proven herself to be a good hunter. I ask you to please not turn her away."

Ashamed of himself for speaking to his father so vehemently, Medicine Paint hung his head, nodded and said, "Áa, yes, Father, I will try."

That had been ten snows ago. Over time, he had lost some of his animosity toward Elk Woman, simply because they hunted together every day and they spoke together and planned their hunts every evening. This alone kept them in one another's company for many hours every day.

It had helped that she often wore boys' clothing when they hunted together, allowing him to pretend she wasn't really a girl. And, despite himself, they had become close; so close were they, he often found he knew her thoughts before she even had a chance to speak them.

Eventually, he had accepted her...except, always at the back of his mind he held a little resentment toward her because she could sometimes best him. Until...

Medicine Paint remembered the day well. Elk Woman had been seventeen, and he twenty and three. It had started out like any other day. They had been hunting upon the wide green plains that day. The morning had yet been young, and he recalled her laughing at him because he'd killed an old bull, whose meat was useless except for its tongue, while she had taken down two young calves, whose meat was entirely good for eating. Of course, he had killed other game besides the old bull, more than she had killed. Yet, her laughter at his expense had grated on him.

It had happened as they were kneeling upon the ground, butchering their kills quickly, knowing that soon the women would follow upon their trail, leading their pack horses to pick up the meat.

He didn't notice at first when the old bull, the one he had assumed was dead, suddenly found life again and rose up onto all four feet. Injured and angered, perhaps out of his mind with pain, the old bull looked forward.

Medicine Paint cast a quick glance at the animal, but saw no immediate harm from the bull, knowing the animal was injured beyond repair and would soon fall again. However, as he continued the butchering of a calf, he saw sudden movement from out of his peripheral vision and beheld the awful sight of the old bull racing toward Elk Woman, who, with her back turned, was unaware of the danger.

Medicine Paint sprung up to his feet and burst into a race against the bull. Could he get to Elk Woman in time? She was some distance ahead of him.

He didn't have a moment in which to think, and, as Medicine Paint sprinted across the plains, he reached behind him for his bow and his arrows which were secured in the quiver upon his back. It was an almost impossible maneuver to grab both bow and arrows given his speed. But, he accomplished it, perhaps because of his need.

The bull was almost upon her when he let his arrow fly, straight at the upper ribs of the bull. The weapon pierced its side, but still the animal raced on. Another arrow quickly followed from his bow, this time aimed directly at the heart of the animal.

Elk Woman had now become aware of the danger, but turning, instead of rising into action, she looked to be frozen in place. Never would Medicine Paint forget the utter look of terror upon her face.

With a cloud of dust and green grass shooting up into the air, the bull crashed to the ground, coming to a halt only a few arms' distance away from the spot where Elk Woman stood frozen. But, Medicine Paint was already in action, and, before the bull had landed, he had run to Elk Woman, had picked her up in his arms as though she were as light as a prairie flower and had sprinted away with her, not stopping until he reached a short tree that stood all alone upon the wide plains.

And, there he stood, holding her body closely against his breast, his arms wound tightly around her. An emotion he didn't recognize rose up within him: he wished to protect her always; he wished to keep her close to him and couldn't imagine ever letting her go.

I love her, he realized all at once. *I have always loved her.* Perhaps this was why he'd always resented her agility in the races, in the hunt and in all the other activities considered to be the realm of a man. For all these years, he had wished to impress her. Yet, he'd been unable to do so because she could accomplish these feats as well as he.

And then, Elk Woman looked up at him with her beautiful dark eyes, and he witnessed a look of such admiration for him, he knew he was hers — had always been hers.

She gasped out, "You saved my life."

He responded to her then in a hoarse voice, saying only, "I did what you would have done for me."

"*Saa,* no. I would have never been able to carry you as you have done with me, carting me along with you while running as though you were in a race with the bull. Nor am I certain I could have hit the animal twice while sprinting as fast as you were. I…I…"

She reached up toward him then and kissed him, and he thought the Creator, Himself, had suddenly endowed him with a joy like no other.

Quickly, he set her feet on the ground, leaned her back against the tree and took control of the kiss.

And, she kissed him back.

As his breath came in quick gasps and his heart beat fast and loudly against his chest, he knew he had better approach her father at once and ask permission to marry her. He would give her father ten of his horses and ask for her hand; her father would say yes, and they would marry and be happy forever.

But, his dream crashed as soon as they returned to camp, Medicine Paint realizing there was a problem, a rather large problem.

No sooner had he and Elk Woman entered the camp when he encountered another young man waiting for her; the man was seeking her hand in marriage. Startled at the unwelcome competition, Medicine Paint held back from asking anything of her father, awaiting Elk Woman's response to the suitor.

That had been thirteen moons ago. At present, as Medicine Paint looked at Elk Woman, he wondered why he'd never really been aware of her natural beauty until that day upon the prairie. And, all this past year, he'd watched as one young man after another had asked for her hand, only to be turned away. Perhaps she would never marry. After all, what need did she have of a man in her life when she could easily obtain her own food? She could probably even enlist one of her sisters to do the cooking and the tanning of skins for her lodge.

What chance did he have?

Still, over this past year, they had continued to hunt together, and always did his gaze linger upon her when he knew she wasn't looking. Now and again, their hands would accidentally touch, and his body would respond to her as though he'd been shot straight in his heart by an arrow.

But, pride kept him from approaching her father to ask for her hand in marriage. What if she were to turn him away as she had the others?

Now, on this bright day in the Moon of Flowers, early summer, the two of them met as they did each morning. Over a quick early meal, Elk Woman told him of her plans, seeking his agreement.

Today she wished to venture into the mountainous glacier country because one of her sisters required the skin of a bighorn sheep. Nothing but the skin from this animal would do for the robe her sister was planning to make. And, since these agile creatures were only to be found within the upper crags of the mountains, this is where Elk Woman said she wished to hunt.

He asked, "You know, of course, of the unpalatable taste of the meat of these creatures?"

"I know," she answered. "Yet, my sister has dreamed of making a robe from the skin of this animal, and we can do much more with the meat and bones. None of it will be wasted."

"Then," he said, "this shall be where we will hunt this day."

She smiled at him, and he looked longingly at her lips until he realized what he was doing and then gazed away from her.

The hunt had gone well this day, and, with the sun beginning its descent into the western sky, they were hurrying back to camp, their pack horse piled with the skins and flesh of their kills. They had barely entered the warm and pleasantly scented grove of elm trees, when suddenly Elk Woman's horse bolted and veered to the left, throwing her to the ground.

Before he could run after her animal, Medicine Paint heard her shout, "A bear! A bear is after me!"

Looking around, Medicine Paint saw the grizzly reaching up to tear at Elk Woman's moccasins as she scrambled up a young tree. But, the tree was no protection; even now it was bending down toward the ground.

As fear engulfed him, he felt his heart sink. It was up to him. And, he knew if he lost her, he would lose himself, also.

Quickly he took out four arrows, placing three of them in his teeth while the other he set against his strong bow. Aiming for the bear's heart, he took care, for the bear was almost upon Elk Woman and his shot had to be perfect.

Whoosh! He let the arrow fly. His aim was true, direct and it pierced straight into the bear's heart. Yet, despite all this, the animal did not fall and instead turned away from its pursuit of Elk Woman to come straight at him.

Though every part of him screamed to turn and run, he forced himself to stand still, and, swiping one of the arrows from where he'd put it in his teeth and placing it directly against his taunt bow string, he let the arrow fly into the bear's eye. Then another and another arrow followed, all aimed at the animal's heart.

Yet, the bear came on and on. Medicine Paint was drawing the last arrow from his quiver when the bear fell over, headfirst. Slowly, with great caution, Medicine Paint approached the bear.

Using his foot, he nudged the animal. It was dead.

Glancing up at Elk Woman to assess any damage done to her, he was surprised to see her running toward him, her pace so quick that when she burst into his arms, she knocked them both to the ground, she landing atop him.

"You…you saved me again! Does this mean you love me? If you do, why have you not asked to marry me? Why do you hesitate? Do you not know how much I love you? As I have always loved you?"

Medicine Paint could hardly believe that what his ears were telling him was true. Did she really love him?

For a moment, he felt incapable of speech. But, after only a short pause, he said, "I have always loved you." He spoke calmly enough, though everything within him was awake and ready to battle again, should the need arise. "I have been afraid to ask for your hand."

"You? Afraid? You, who have risked your life to shoot a bull and a bear so I might live, expect me to believe you have been afraid to ask for me as your woman?"

He grinned up at her. "I have feared your lack of love for me more than the most dangerous of all animals."

She laughed, then said, "My father will be happy to cease having to turn away all my suitors."

"He will? He is aware of your love? Of mine?"

"Of course! He knows I have been waiting for you all my life. Only you. It has always been you."

And, then it happened. Medicine Paint laughed and laughed until his ribs hurt, and then, turning Elk Woman over so she lay beneath him, he kissed her with all the pent-up passion and love in his heart.

After a while, they gathered together their horses and paced slowly back to camp. And, as the sun set into a red-and-golden burst in the western sky, they walked casually into camp, and all those who saw them were glad to see that these two were holding hands.

It is said Medicine Paint and Elk Woman lived long and happy lives and had many children. Indeed, all the people rejoiced to witness, at last, these two brave people had come together as one.

Yes, the tribe would go on.

THE END

Red Hawk and the Mermaid

For: Ariana and Lila

Indian Territory

The Southern Blackfoot Pikuni Tribe

1850's

Setting down her trowel, Effie, who was eight years old, knew the time had come for a break. She exhaled deeply and, straightening up, wiped her brow of perspiration. Having helped her parents at the site of the archaeological dig throughout the early morning hours, she had done her duty, at least for a while. It was time for a bath.

"I am so hot," she whined. She started to pout, but then thought better of her actions, and in a more adult voice asked, "May I go swimming?"

With a quick nod and a sweet smile, her mother endorsed the action. She did advise, however, "Stay close. It's still quite hazy out this morning, and I don't want you missing a step and falling."

"I won't do that, and I will stay close." Immediately Effie's spirits lifted. If there was one thing Effie liked most about accompanying her mother and father on these excavations, it was the sense of freedom she enjoyed. No one—outside of Lesley—treated her as if she were too young to know her own mind. And perhaps it was in response to her parents' trust that Effie behaved herself uncommonly well.

Tantrums were an unknown affair. Truth be told, Effie considered herself as adult as the next person. She was simply trapped inside a child's body.

"Is Lesley going with you?" her mother asked.

"No. She left with one of Father's students, someone named William, I think. They said they were going to survey the lay of the land."

"Oh. That's nice."

Effie sighed. "Yes, Mother. Now may I go swimming?"

"Of course, dear."

"Thank you."

Deciding to leave before her mother changed her mind or asked more questions, Effie padded toward her favorite spot. She could almost see the place from the excavation site.

Caught off to the side of the Big River—the Missouri River—was a splendid water hole. Not too deep, not too shallow, the place was hidden from view by long, green prairie grasses, as well as pine, cottonwoods and a magnificent willow. In the distance—and able to be seen from the pool on most days—were white-capped mountains, which favored the land with a fairytale appeal. It was the ideal place for a quick dip.

Effie knew it was dangerous to swim alone—and briefly she wished that Lesley were a little more friendly toward her, for it would be fun to have a swimming companion. But Lesley's attitude in regards to Effie was far from amicable, except of course when Lesley wanted something.

Perhaps Lesley thought Effie too young. Certainly, Effie was the younger by four years. But in attitude, Effie considered herself to be the more mature of the two of them. Lesley exhibited more tantrums than Effie had ever witnessed in anyone.

As Effie treaded toward the water, she couldn't help but notice the profusion of pink wildflowers whose fragrances filled the air with a sweet scent. She touched their soft, dewy petals as she passed by them, her fingers coming away wet from the encounter.

Odd, in places this morning the fog was so thick she could barely see her hand as she flattened it over the grasses and flowers. But in other areas, the haze was starting to dissipate, lending to the land a cathedral-like profusion of golden streams of light slanting through the mist.

For an instant, Effie caught her breath, so beautiful was the sight—so profound. The moment felt sacred, as though she were close to something…something wonderful. Perhaps it was the Creator that she felt so near to, since such beauty could not be by accident.

She let out her breath. It was a good way to start the day, and as she stripped off her dress, her petticoats and chemise, throwing them to the side, peace filled her soul. She left her square-toed boots on her feet so her tender toes need not tread on any sharp rocks. Her pantalettes also remained in place, since she couldn't bring herself to strip to bare skin from the waist down. Her drawers were green, not white, as a woman's pantalettes might be. Green, because her mother had made them from the canvas-like material of an old tent.

At last Effie was ready to swim, and unafraid, she waded into the water.

In truth, there was little need for fear. The swimming hole was close to her parents' dig, well within earshot, were there to be any trouble. And Effie was an experienced swimmer, her parents having schooled her in the techniques of lifesaving when she was so young she could barely crawl. Thus, Effie felt safe and quite exuberant.

The water was only ankle deep at the shoreline, but it was cool and refreshing, as she had known it would be. Soon, Effie plunged into the water completely, wetting herself from the top of her very red head to the bottom of her heavy, wet boots. Surfacing, she grinned.

What pleasure!

****

As twelve-year-old Red Hawk treaded a path to the water, a few rays of golden sunlight pushed their way through the fog. In response, the ground came alive, welcoming the warmth of those beams. Here, and as far as the eye could see, the lush, green earth was covered with a misty haze. Mother Earth was awakening.

The early morning scents of grass and pine were bursting with aroma, sweetening the atmosphere. The terrain was solid and firm beneath Red Hawk's feet, and the air enveloped the boy in a cool embrace. But Red Hawk barely noticed the earth and all her scents and secrets, so inward was his attention.

He was confused.

This was to be his last day in camp. On the morrow, he would awaken, never to see Grandfather or any of the people again, unless he was successful in lifting the curse, which plagued his people. Though Red Hawk had often wished for this very opportunity, the reality of it was more than he could easily assimilate.

He would have eighteen years in which to break the curse. Surely, he could accomplish this. To his young mind, it seemed like a great deal of time had been allotted him.

However, if that were true, why was the spell proving to be so hard for others to break? So many champions before him had tried; so many failures.

Would he be successful? He certainly hoped he would be, although without even starting his mission, he was disadvantaged, for his heart longed to seek revenge for the deaths of his mother and father. But alas, this was not to be his fate. The welfare of the tribe now depended on him.

"Remember Grandfather in all things," he muttered to himself. "Remember Grandfather."

And so it was that Red Hawk was grumbling when he saw her.

There, sitting on a rock at the edge of the pool, was the most unusual but perhaps the most beautiful creature he had ever witnessed. He stared. Was she a vision?

She could be, for he was unable to see the girl as well as he might. The ever-present mist that swirled around her made her appear dreamlike. Yet, for some unknown reason, he felt certain she was real.

Was she part fish?

No, she must be human. She looked human…well, at least she did from the waist up. But she was certainly like no other being he had ever seen. For one thing, her hair was a dark shade of red, not black or brown, and the locks of her mane were curling about her head in cascading spirals. Her skin color was a shade or two whiter than that to which he was accustomed, but not enough to draw a great deal of notice.

From her waist upward, she wore nothing, but this seemed a usual sort of happenstance. Most of the children in the village ran naked, and she was a child, he determined, since, from his view of her, she had thus far developed nothing that due to modesty must be hidden.

But...did she have legs?

Red Hawk couldn't be certain. From the waist downward, it appeared she no longer grew skin. All he could see from there down was green. Surely most forms of human beings were not green on the bottom, were they?

Was she a white person? Had there not been rumors in the tribe about such people? Stories that the tribal medicine man, White Claw, had seen such people and had talked to them? Were white people half fish?

Slowly, as silently as he could, Red Hawk crept toward the girl and was almost upon her when she moved, stretching. Her hands came up to push back her hair, as though she were combing it with her fingers.

Without warning, she turned toward him. Her eyes were big, a light shade of brown, and she stared straight at him.

He froze.

She grinned.

What happened then Red Hawk could never explain, nor did he ever wish to. One moment he was on his feet, the next he was tripping all over himself. Suddenly he was all hands and legs, and they seemed to be going in all directions at once. The result of course was that he landed on the ground none too delicately, and quite on his rump.

"Hello," she said, when things had settled down. "Who are you?"

Red Hawk had no conception of what the words meant that she spoke, or even if those words were part of a language. Was she singing? She might be; her voice was that beautiful.

Looking up at her, for he had yet to arise, he voiced, "*Oki,*" deciding that it was best to greet her politely.

She frowned, clearly not educated in the great language of his people.

"Who are you?" she repeated. However, since he didn't understand her, and vice versa, he used sign language to help impart his meaning.

Yet, even in this, a most basic form of communication, she appeared to be adrift, for she continued to frown at him. Obviously, she did not understand him or what he said. The scowl on her face lasted but a moment, as though it were unable to take permanent hold on one so bright and cheery, and very soon the grimace had transformed into an easy smile.

Maybe that was his undoing. The grin. It was said that there were people whose faces glowed when they smiled, as though lit from within with magic.

She might be such a one, for when Red Hawk looked into her eyes, he thought that surely he had eaten something bad this day. His innards were awash in butterflies.

"Well, no matter who you are," said the girl after a while, "would you like to swim with me?" She bestowed upon him yet another of those beguiling grins.

He froze, gaping. He knew of nothing else to do but stare at her.

When he didn't respond to her question at once, she made hand motions at him, giving him to understand that she was about to fly into the air…or at least that was what he thought she said.

Was she a goddess, then?

He frowned at her, and she giggled, and, with a single hand motion, she invited him to join her. Then, as quick as all that, she slipped into the water.

Was he to follow? Was she a water being after all?

Blackfeet legends told of such beings. There were said to be nymphs, sometimes monsters, who were sent from the water's depths only to lure a man to his death.

Perhaps she was such a one. Mayhap he should use caution.

Red Hawk, however, ignored any prudence. He was curious about her because she was…different. Besides, though he was only twelve winters old, at this moment he felt very much the male of the species.

With nary a thought for personal danger, he followed the girl into the water. If she were a siren leading him to his death, why would some men fear it?

But she wasn't about death, he soon came to understand. She was about playing…and fun. And there was no great need to translate languages when the object of the game was to decide who was "it".

"Catch me," she said, as she tagged him with the slightest brush of her hand. She dove underwater, then he followed her, letting her take the lead.

She is not a fish, he saw at last, as he opened his eyes underwater. *Nor is she a siren, or a goddess.*

She swam by use of hands and legs, not fins. What he had thought might have been scales from her waist down were nothing more than the ugliest sort of leggings he had ever seen.

Why would a girl swim in such things? And with her footgear still on? He was dressed only in his breechcloth.

Catching up with her, he tagged her.

Still underwater, she spun around, and though they were both beneath the surface, she smiled at him. Then, as quick as that, she lunged toward him, her arm extended.

He backed up, but his heart wasn't into retreating from her, and he let her touch him. Her hand was soft, delicate, and he was pondering the experience, when all at once she struck out, away from him.

They both surfaced.

"I am the better swimmer of the two of us," she taunted him, before she giggled. Though Red Hawk couldn't discern the words, her meaning was clear. She was playing to win.

He realized his mistake at once. If he were to earn her respect, he would have to prevail in this game. However, he was wise enough to realize that he should not shove defeat at her too soon. *Saa*, he would need to win this game with her blessing and goodwill. Not an easy feat for a boy of twelve.

"*Kika*, wait," he called out in the Blackfeet tongue. "*Poohsapoot*, come here! Let us define this game."

She paid him no heed, and not because she didn't understand him, language barrier or not.

He followed her, tagged her, but he didn't at once retreat. Instead, opening his arms, he invited her to touch him back. To this end, he swam around her, leaping to and fro, but always at her arm's length.

Tentatively, doubtfully, she reached out toward him. She had almost grazed him again when he extended his hands toward her instead. He tickled her.

"No fair." She laughed, doubling up. "Your arms are longer than mine. Now, no tickling."

He didn't understand her words, though he was fairly certain he comprehended exactly what she wanted. Grinning at her, he repeated the action.

"No!" she said, and there was no mistaking the intent of that word. He wasn't about to end the game, however, not yet, and so he danced around her once again, his arms wide open and tempting her to make him "it".

"What are you doing?" Her gaze followed him as he swam easily around her.

He didn't answer. Instead, he tugged at one of her curls.

"Stop that," she ordered sharply. Nonetheless, she was giggling.

He repeated the action.

"Oh, this is not fair. You are bigger than I am and your arms are longer." She leaped toward him suddenly. He backed away, just in time, his arms still open as he treaded water, offering her a clear target.

She laughed, and he joined in with her.

And so it was that the morning hours wore on. Back and forth they played, Red Hawk allowing the beautiful water spirit to win the game of tag. But never more than he.

"Oh, you are too much for me." She smiled up at him. "Unfortunately, I must pronounce you the winner, though I think you have a terrible advantage over me." As if to compensate for the inequality, she reached down in the water and pulled off each of her shoes in turn. "Why did I not think of this before now? These awful pantalettes I am wearing get in my way and my boots drag me down, while you have only your breechcloth to restrict you. No wonder you are able to taunt me."

Taking aim, she threw first one boot at the shoreline, and then the other. Her hurl wasn't accurate, and one by one, each shoe fell short of the shore, plopping into the water, the hard leather causing them to sink swiftly. At once gallant, Red Hawk propelled himself forward, capturing one shoe, then the other.

She followed, wading right up to him, where she extended her hand, asking for the boots. Slowly he presented the shoes to their owner, his hand lingering over the last boot before dropping his arm to his side.

"Thank you," she said, looking up at him. Smiling, she held her shoes against her breast and pointed to herself. "Effie. Can you say that? Effie." Again she indicated herself.

"Eh-h-h—eee," he repeated.

She nodded. "Close enough. And you are?" She pointed toward him.

Words and gestures aside, he knew instinctively what she asked, but it was beyond his means to tell her what she desired. Somewhat alarmed—for an Indian would never ask another his name—Red Hawk tried to justify her action. She was not from here, he decided. She might not know the protocols of his polite society.

For one, a man never spoke his name aloud. Not only was it a taboo, it was also considered boastful, for names often told of great deeds.

Also, Red Hawk was reluctant to willingly utter the name that the others in the Clan called him. His name was Red Hawk, not Poor Orphan. Even if she wouldn't understand the words, he could not bring himself to say them.

He gazed away from her, prompting her to try again. Pointing to him, she said, "And you are?"

This time Red Hawk shrugged and, turning away, presented her with his back as he swam toward the middle of the pond. There he waited, motioning her forward, asking her with signs to continue their game.

She shook her head. "Aren't you going to tell me your name? After we have spent such a remarkable morning together? What am I to call you?"

Red Hawk feigned misunderstanding, saying nothing.

"Oh, very well," she uttered, clearly exasperated. "It's not very much to ask, though, is it? I'd just like to know what to say if I'm to address you. Will you be here tomorrow?"

Again, he remained silent, not understanding her words, though he did try to get her to join him once more in the center of the pool.

She shook her head. Spinning away from him, she began to wade closer to the shoreline. "I can't. Don't misunderstand me. It's not because you won't tell me your name or anything, but my parents might become concerned if I am gone too long. Already I've been here a few hours, and so I must return to them. I have enjoyed your company, though." With a grin that was half apology, she turned to leave the water.

A feeling of loss swept over Red Hawk, and he swam toward her, following her. Coming up behind her, he touched her gently on the shoulder to get her attention, then taking hold of her hand, he guided it to his shoulder, where he allowed her to "tag" him.

Averting his gaze, Red Hawk started to draw back from her, but she held on to him tightly. Curious, his glance met hers, became lost in hers.

"I have enjoyed my morning swim with you," she said earnestly, the honest appeal in her eyes intriguing. At last, she let go of him and, reaching her hands up behind her neck, she unfastened the necklace she wore — one made of a gold-colored substance. After placing the necklace in her small hand, she extended the jewelry toward him.

"Take it," she said, when Red Hawk didn't immediately stretch out his hand to capture it. "Take it," she repeated, motioning toward it and then to him.

At length, he nodded and grasped hold of the prize.

"There," she said, "that wasn't so hard, was it?"

But he didn't understand her meaning as the words were not easily discerned.

Looking down at himself, as he stood before her in only his breechcloth, he searched his body for a gift he might give her.

But what? There was little that he owned.

Time seemed short as he pondered the problem, and he had almost given up the idea altogether, when he remembered...his earrings. The white shell earrings he wore were of some value.

Once they had been his mother's. Now they would be hers.

After unfastening them, he placed the two white shells in his palm and extended his hand toward her.

"For me?" she said, and he nodded.

Her tiny fingers slid over his palm as she drew near to take the prize. Red Hawk was amazed that a simple touch should make him feel as if he were suddenly falling through space.

"I don't know why I should say this to you," she said, "for I know that you cannot understand me—and perhaps that is why I feel I *must* say this—but I think I have fallen in love with you." Her hand briefly clasped his.

And then it was over. She turned away and hurried off in a direction opposite to that of his camp. She was almost out of sight when she stopped still and spun back around.

Running toward him, she came right up to him and said, "I almost forgot." Standing on the tips of her toes, she brought her face up to his, where she placed a kiss on his cheek. She giggled. "I hope to see you here tomorrow." Flashing him one last grin, she fled.

She didn't look back, and maybe it was good she hadn't. For, in response to that kiss, slight though it was, Red Hawk had taken a few quick steps toward her as if to reciprocate, when suddenly he became so uncoordinated he tripped over himself.

Once again, the earth cushioned his fall. Once again, he lay flat on his fanny.

Though she had not spared Red Hawk a final glance, he watched her, looking at the place where she had disappeared for a long time, as though her impression still remained there.

"*Otahkohsoa' tsis*, Red Hawk," he said to the air, as if it might carry his words to her. "Red Hawk is my name."

Slowly he came up to his feet and stepped toward the water, where he looked out upon the place where they had played. Would she come here tomorrow, hoping to see him? For a moment, if a moment only, he wished this duty to his people had not been forced upon him.

He would like nothing better than to see her again, and to frolic with her as though the world were without cares. Indeed, although he was too young to know about matters of the heart, he felt certain that he had fallen in love with this water spirit, the girl who had called herself Effie.

"Eff…ee," he murmured, and as he turned away from the water to step back toward his encampment, he was struck with the idea that somehow, in some way, he would see her again.

The thought caused him to smile.

THE END

Moon Wolf and Miss Alice

For Lila, Lucas and Ari

Historical Note

The following historical background will hopefully be of some help in understanding this story. The time is around 1857 and the place is the Montana Territory.

Gold was discovered near Bannack, Montana. Because of this discovery, many, many people who hadn't previously lived in Montana suddenly decided to make the Montana Territory their home. Mostly it was unmarried men who came to this northern land, and it is noted in several books that these men were dishonest and were known liars. The book, *The Blackfeet: Raiders on the Northwestern Plains by John C. Ewers*, writes that these newcomers were little more than "thieves and blackguards," the sort of persons who could "not be tolerated in any civilized society."

Of course with this kind of person suddenly coming to live in Montana, many wrongs began to happen to the American Indians. Because the Blackfeet people had fought the American Military and had lost, many of these wrongs went unpunished.

Treaties were promises between both the American Indians and the United States Government. They were oaths sworn to, and were never to be broken. But one by one the American Government began to break the promises made in those Treaties. Even food promised to the Blackfeet people went missing, creating problems, and causing harm to some of the Blackfeet people.

Sadly, those who were supposed to keep the Treaties in good order (these people were called Indian Agents), began to justify (make excuses for) acts of violence against the Blackfeet people. The Blackfeet people's hearts became sad.

The Blackfeet people began to despair (despair means to be sad and think there is no future). It was during this time that the American Military forts began to set up schools. These schools should have been a very good thing. But they weren't.

Instead of teaching the Indians to read and write, the

schools were used to try to change the American Indian child and teach him or her things that would not help him in his life. Also, the schools often took children away from their homes. Sometimes there was fighting in the schools. And sometimes there were teachers who came from far-away places who thought it was right to use punishment, instead of helping the student.

It is during this bad time period in Montana history that our story begins.

Prologue

Blackfeet Reservation

Montana

Early 1900s

"Sit down, my grandchildren, and I will tell you a story."

The youngsters, laughing and giggling, crowded in through the tepee's entryway, its flap, which served as a door, thrown back to allow access. Several women, the children's mothers, were at work in the sunshine; the men were out tending to their livestock and horses.

Smoke from the lodge's inner fire found its way under the worn, yet colorful tepee lining, the sooty fragrance curling its way up and out of the upper opening, the "ears" of the home. But there the similarity between this lodge and the lodges of old ended, for no longer were the riches of Indian life to be seen there.

Spread out on the ground, underneath where the

old man sat, laid a three-point trade blanket and several other quilts, each lining the floor. These, and the single medicine bundle hanging from the inner lining, remained the only evidence of the once powerful Blackfeet confederation.

"What story are you going to tell us today, Grandfather?"

The old man smiled kindly at the pretty little girl whose dark eyes sparkled with life, a flair in them reminding him of the former, wild life of the Indian; a life he had loved well. He motioned the child to come toward him, noting in doing so, that the child's features mirrored the spirits of her ancestors. If only she knew.

The child flopped down next to him and he drew her closer, grinning at the small girl who sat so trustingly beside him. Then he gestured toward the other children, inviting them to sit.

It was time, he decided; time to tell these youngsters the great stories of their fathers, stories that the new government agents now forbid. Tales he hoped these youngsters would never forget.

Áa, he said, a Blackfeet word that means, yes. This was good. He set his head back and shut his eyes.

He remembered the past very well. It had happened in a time before the newcomers had invaded their country so thoroughly, a brief time before the reservation days; an age when the Indian had still roamed free. (A reservation is a section of land or country that has been set aside for the Indians.)

Taking a deep breath, he began, "My children, today I will tell you a story about a great warrior, a brave young boy who helped his sister."

"Alone, Grandfather?"

"*Áa*, yes, alone. Now listen well and I will tell you about a moment in history when the newcomers to this land had just begun to live next to our people...a day when the people's future was to change..."

Chapter One

Fort Benton on the Missouri River
1857, Northwest Territory

"Two and two equals...?" The teacher slapped the ruler against the blackboard, the sound of the *wap* of the wooden stick an unspoken threat. The teacher—who had only recently arrived here—stood frowning, arms crossed at her waist. "Young lady," the teacher threatened as she took a step forward and unfolded her arms, "answer me."

The young Indian girl, standing at the front of the class, didn't make a sound. Head down, she stared at her feet.

Looking at the child, who was no older than herself, Alice Clayton felt as if her heart might break. Personally, she had never understood why the wild Indians had been brought to this school. Her mother said the whole matter was an experiment by their Indian agent, Alfred J. Vaughan, to see if the Indians could be civilized, whatever that meant.

But the whole thing was doomed to failure because Indians didn't learn from this kind of teaching.

At least that's what her mother had told her: that the Indians of the plains had not been brought up with the same books and stories as she had; that the Indians had their own legends and tales, their own way of teaching and of doing things. Indians were close to the land, were free, or at least they were supposed to be. Alice's mother had also said, and Alice agreed, that the Indians would be better off if left independent which, Alice decided, must mean "left alone."

So, if all these things were true, why was their teacher making an example of this poor child? What did it matter if the girl could or could not add the two plus two on the chalkboard? Alice knew that if she were to approach the girl and promise her four beads while giving her only three, the young girl would know the difference.

Alice saw tears streaming down the youngster's face as she endured not only the silent threat of the teacher, but the sneers and scoffing of her "fellow classmates" too.

Something should be done. Such dealings were not right. Yet Alice felt helpless. She was only eight years old, a child herself. What good was she against a teacher — against the bad words of the others?

Oh, no. Alice caught her breath.

The teacher — an overly skinny and sickly-looking woman — had raised the ruler in her hand as though she might hit the girl. It caused the youngster to put a hand over her eyes, as though to shield them against harm.

Then the worst happened. Down came the ruler, down across the Indian girl's arm.

The child didn't cry out, didn't even move a muscle, although she did whimper as tears fell down over her face.

The teacher shouted out a few more terrible words. Still the young girl remained silent.

"I'll teach you to talk back to me," the teacher hissed, while Alice tried to make sense of what the teacher had said. The young girl hadn't uttered a word.

Wap! Another slap across the girl's arms. The teacher raised her arm for another blow.

It never came.

In a blur of buckskin and feathers, a young Indian boy, the same one who had been at their school for about a week, burst forward into the classroom, putting himself between the youngster and the teacher. In his hand, he held a knife.

The class went from a mass of jeers and name-calling to sudden silence.

Where had the boy come from? And the knife? Where had he gotten that? It was well known that the wild Indians, even the children, had all of their weapons taken from them when they came into the fort.

Yet there was no mistaking that knife in his hand, nor the boy's intent.

Good, thought Alice.

Immediately, the teacher backed up, but, in doing so, she tripped over a wastebasket, losing her balance. She fell backwards into the trash can, bottom first.

Alice couldn't help herself. She laughed.

It was the only sound to be heard in an otherwise silent classroom. No one looked at her, however. Everyone appeared...stunned.

The teacher's face filled with a red color, her hands were clenched over the top of the basket. "You...you savage. You pushed me—"

"This one," the Indian responded, pointing to himself, "has not touched you. But give me good reason to"—he waved his knife in front of her—"and I will."

The teacher spat even more ugly words, before she uttered loudly, "I'll have your skin for this, young man."

"Humph." The boy approached the teacher, then said, "And I will have your hair."

It took a moment for his meaning to register, but as the boy swung out his knife, taking hold of the teacher's tight bun, she screamed.

Whack! Off came the bun, harmlessly falling into the youngster's hand.

"You heathen, why, I'll..." In an almost superhuman effort, the teacher jumped up, out of the basket. The boy went into action at once. He grabbed hold of the Indian girl and, pulling her after him, ran toward the classroom's only window.

That was all it took for the other youngsters in the room to come alive. Insults and threats could be heard all through the early morning air, while the two outcasts made the best escape they could. Boys, almost all of them having some mixture of American Indian heritage in their blood, sprang up from their chairs, leaping after the two runaways, who had by this time cleared the window.

The entire school cleared out, as student after student bolted from out the door or the window, chasing after the pair.

Alice, however, arose from her seat at a slower pace, walking thoughtfully toward the doorway of the tiny cabin which served as the schoolhouse. Fingering her soft brownish-red curls as she moved, she decided to go home. It seemed that school had been let out for the day.

Poor Indian kids. Wasn't it enough that the children had been taken away from their family to be "educated"? According to her mother, the townspeople weren't making it easy on these wild ones either, saying bad words to them and making fun of them. Who would want to stay? Alice asked herself.

Her thoughts troubled, Alice began to make a path toward her home.

Chapter Two

Her house was made of wood and was one of the nicer homes in the fort. It stood toward the back of the town. It was set away from the river, and was isolated from the rest of the fort. It was a quiet spot; it was also a location that her father had personally selected before he had left to go back East, almost four years ago.

Her mother was well-to-do, and many years ago, she had helped to found this town, right alongside her father. It should have given her mother the right to speak her point of view on matters of concern. But it didn't, because the military ruled the fort, and a single woman's voice went unnoticed.

As Alice made her way through the fort, she wondered what her mother would say about what had happened this day, knowing that it was her mother's nature to blame the townspeople, not the Indians. Hadn't her mother often commented on the unkind behavior of a few people in this town? Hadn't Alice herself observed that those here in the fort, often made up the ills they complained about?

Why? Alice Clayton could little understand it.

She only wished there were something she could do, some way to help. If only she knew where the two Indians were right now, she would offer them kindness and hope. Yes, she decided. She would be kind to them, make friends with them, show them that they could trust her.

Why, she would...

What was that? There it was again, a glimpse of something from out of the corner of her eye. Buckskin, feathers—two small arms and legs? There in the bushes? She turned to take a closer look.

The Indian boy and his knife suddenly appeared out of nowhere. He pressed the knife close against her throat, and a hand covered her mouth as his arms slipped about her waist. He dragged her backward, toward that bush.

"You cry out...I kill you," his threatened.

Alice looked up into a set of the deepest, blackest eyes she had ever seen. She nodded. It was all she could think of to do. She could only hope that she might be given the chance to prove to him that she was a friend.

If only he would let her…

Chapter Three

The dusty scent of the boy's skin, the dirt on his hands were practically all that Alice could breathe, and she thought she might gag. It wasn't that the smell was unpleasant, it was more that he held her mouth too tightly. She squirmed.

"Be still."

Two young boys flew past them, and more footsteps followed. More of the same followed, the pounding of boots, of adult feet striking the ground was all that could be heard. All of these people were rushing by them without seeing them.

Alice struggled in the boy's grip. She wanted to let him know that she was a friend, that she would help him. It was useless, however. The boy held his hand too tightly over her lips.

Gunshots in the distance caught Alice's attention, and then came more shouts and hurrying footsteps. Gunshots? Surely no one intended to cause physical harm to these two, did they?

She had to do something. Quickly, Alice took stock of where she was. Over to her right was her home — within running distance — and beside her house was the secret place, that place known only to Alice and her mother.

It was a special place, a part of Alice's inheritance that might prove to be the cause of saving the lives of these two outcasts, if she could only make them understand. Could she?

She had to try. Motioning toward the house, Alice pointed at the two Indians, then flapped her hands like wings, trying to show an image of birds, flying away free. Would he understand?

The young boy followed her hand motions for a moment, then tugged at her to remain still. He looked away.

Alice tried again. Point to the house, to the Indians, a bird flying away free. Once more, over and over. It took a few more times of doing the same thing before the boy frowned, looking down at Alice, at her hands, at the house.

More voices, more footsteps coming toward them.

Alice gestured again.

With a stern frown at her, the boy loosened his grip, allowing Alice to whisper, "I know a secret way out of the fort."

Would he believe her? Did he understand she meant to help him?

Dark eyes glared into her own.

"It's at the side of my home." She motioned toward the house.

"There is nothing there, white girl; a house, a wall, no more. Do you try to trap us?"

Alice didn't say a word. And perhaps it was her silence that saved her.

He asked, "How we escape there?"

"In our root cellar," Alice was quick to answer, "my mother's and mine. There is a hidden tunnel."

"Where is this...root cellar?"

Alice pointed to a set of bushes that almost, but not quite, hid the wooden doors of the cellar. "There," she said. "See it? It goes down to a passage underground. It's like a cave. It leads to the hills."

She could see him hesitate, watched as indecision played across his features. At last, though, he said, "You show us."

Alice nodded.

They waited until the approaching footsteps faded away. Then he gave her a push forward, and she fled as fast as her small legs would carry her, on and on toward the side of her yard, with the two Indians following close behind.

"Here." She pushed her way into the bushes and pulled at the doors of the cellar. They wouldn't give. She almost cried.

The Indian boy came to her rescue, tugging on the doors and hauling them up.

"Hurry." She motioned to the two of them to enter. Quickly, they did as she had asked, and they fled down some small steps that led into the cellar. Alice followed them, and dragged the doors shut behind her. Instantly, all was darkness inside, but it didn't bother Alice. She merely sighed in relief.

"This is trap," the boy said, his knife coming once more to Alice's neck. Maybe he didn't like the darkness, Alice thought.

"No," she insisted, unafraid. "I'll show you."

Lifting a rug on the floor, Alice uncovered a small

mound made of mud and earth. Brushing the dirt away, Alice pointed to a trapdoor the dirt had hidden.

Pulling up on the door, she glanced toward the boy, barely able to make out his features in the darkness.

"Come," she said and she dropped down to the ladder. Down and down she climbed, her two charges following after her.

Plunging to the stone floor of the cavern below, Alice fumbled in the dark until she found the lantern her mother always kept there. Checking first to make sure that it was working properly, she lit the wick in the lantern with matches that were always kept on a ledge. Instantly light flooded throughout the cave. Instinctively, she took the hand of the Indian boy.

"Hold hands," she instructed, and she began to lead the two of them through the tunnels. The darkness of the caves, their earthy smells and their coolness had never bothered Alice. They were a part of her family, a part of her.

She and her mother came here often, hunting a treasure that had been lost here long ago. Although if Alice were honest, she would admit that sometimes she sought out the comfort of the caves for pleasure alone, these caverns being a legacy to her from her father.

"If you lead us back to...that village, white girl, I will kill you."

"I know." Alice hesitated. "But I won't. I promise you."

He let out a snort. "The promise of a white girl."

"The word of Alice Clayton." She might not be aware of it, but Alice lifted her chin. "Not all white people are bad."

He didn't say a word, though another menacing growl escaped from his throat.

Well, what did it matter anyway? She would show him. Wasn't it what her mother always told her, that actions, not words, were important? It took an hour or so of careful travel, but she didn't falter in her step. She knew the way to the outlet that led to the hills.

She had already decided that she would show him he was wrong about her and about her people. And so it would be, if she had anything to do with it...

Chapter Four

The tunnel climbed slowly, gradually upward, until at last, up ahead, she could see light, hear the rush of the waterfall that stood at the outside entrance to the caves.

Ah, the great falls. This was her most favorite spot in the world. It lay apart from the fort; it was untouched and unspoiled. No one else knew of the caverns or the beauty of these cliffs either, as far as she knew, since they were hidden on all sides by the height of the hills. At least, Alice silently corrected herself, no other white man knew of them.

Alice led the young boy and the girl underneath the falls, out onto the rocks and into the bright sunshine outside, allowing the two young people to adjust their eyesight to the light before she stated, "I don't know where your people are, but I reckon you'll be able to find them from here."

The boy looked around him and inhaled a deep breath before he glanced back at Alice. He stared at her.

Then, without any expression on his face whatsoever, he murmured, "What strange manner is this? A white girl who keeps her word?"

Alice stiffened her spine before she responded, "I told you I would."

He nodded. "So you did, white girl, so you did."

The young Indian miss at his side didn't seem as lacking in emotion as the boy, however, and she came up to Alice and gave her a big hug. Then she said something to Alice in a very strange language.

The lad translated, "She says something good will come to you."

Alice nodded, smiling. Then it occurred to her. "She doesn't speak English?"

"*Saa*, no."

"So she could not even understand the teacher?"

The boy remained silent, though when he gazed down at Alice, he suddenly smiled. It was the first cheerful emotion Alice had seen on his face. The action made him look younger still, innocent, and oh, so very handsome. Alice gaped up at him, as she admired his long dark hair that fell back from his face. The cooling breeze from the falls brought tiny droplets to his tanned skin; his dark eyes, surprisingly full of approval for her, watched her closely. Alice couldn't help herself. Gazing back, she felt as though she fell under his spell.

Slowly, the boy took a piece of jewelry from around his neck. A round, single white shell dangled from a chain of bleached-white buckskin. He drew it over Alice's head and settled it around her neck.

"*Soka'pii,* good." His right hand signed the meaning of the Blackfeet word in a single gesture. "Looks good on you."

With the tip of his finger, he tilted her face up toward his. "I will remember you always, young white girl, and what you have done for me and my sister."

So, thought Alice, the Indian girl was his sister. Pleased by the realization, she said, pointing to herself, "Alice."

"Aa-lees," the young lad rolled her name smoothly over on his tongue.

She pointed to him. "And your name is?"

He shook his head. "A warrior does not speak his own name. To do so would be dishonorable."

"But I would like to know..."

She was interrupted by the boy saying something to his sister, again in that strange language.

With a quick glance up at Alice, the Indian girl spoke, and, pointing to her brother, said, *"Ki'somm-makoyi."*

"Ki'somm-makoyi," Alice whispered. "That is your name?"

He nodded.

"What does it mean?"

"I cannot say."

"Please?"

He took a deep breath, grinned at her slightly, then said, pointing to himself, "This one is called Moon Wolf."

"Moon Wolf."

Another nod.

She smiled up at him. "Moon Wolf, I will never forget you."

He stared into her eyes, his look serious, before he volunteered, "Come with us, young Aa-lees. Come with us and I promise that when we grow older, I will take you for wife and show you great honor for what you have done for us this day."

Alice might have chuckled at the suggestion, for the

thought was silly. He was much too young to speak of such a thing. And she was much too young to hear it.

Yet there was a quietness and a determination in his words that she couldn't discount. "I cannot," she replied, her voice sounding adult to her ears. "I would bring you more trouble if I went with you. No one in the fort would rest until I was found."

He inclined his head. "That is true. For a small girl, you speak with wise tongue. But still," his chin shot up in the air, "no matter what others would do, I would honor you in this way."

His words, or perhaps the pride in his manner, reached out to her, its effect on her serious, and she felt herself responding to the boy, tears of respect for him, maybe even joy, coming to her eyes. She said, "I cannot go with you. My mother would miss me too much."

He remained silent for many moments before he nodded at last. "So it will be," he uttered, "but know that though you choose to stay behind, I will carry your image with me, here," he held his hand to his heart, "for so long as this one should live. And should we ever meet again, I promise that I will marry you."

Alice stared. These were strong words, a powerful

vow for a boy not much older than she, and Alice stared up at him in silence for several seconds, afraid to move lest she spoil the moment. Slowly, he brought his hand up to run his fingers over her cheek, his touch gentle. Carefully, he traced the path of her tears with a finger, before bringing that same finger to his own cheek.

"And now," he whispered to her, touching that finger that was still wet with her tears to his eye, "a part of you is a part of me."

He didn't wait for her to respond. All at once, he turned and fled, disappearing, along with his sister down the rocks and out onto the open and wide countryside.

Alice fingered her cheek for what seemed like forever, letting the warmth of the sunshine wash over her and dry her face. In the distance she could hear the birds sing, while closer at hand, she could smell the perfumed scent of the grasses and wildflowers. Lightly, the wind ruffled her hair, lifting her spirit gently upward until she felt herself becoming a part of all this, a part of the natural way of things.

She would never forget this, never forget him. She couldn't.

Alice had become, in the space of a moment, charmed by him. She had fallen in love with him; a love that would last her a lifetime, she thought, no matter the state of her youth. And in that instant, she knew her life would change its course for better.

She would meet him again sometime in the future. She was certain of it. Moreover, she had learned a lesson this day: she had learned that greatness came from the heart. Heroes or heroines were heroes or heroines not because of the color of their skin, but because of the goodness in their heart.

She would never forget.

Epilogue

"She was right," said the old, story-teller. "They did meet again. They did marry, and they both lived to a very great age. Always was their love for one another a thing of beauty and inspiration for all the people. They had many children and grandchildren, some living to this day. Some, who are sitting here beside me, are direct descendants from those two heroes.

"But, come, when I started this story, I told you that there was only one hero. Do you see now that there were two?"

"Yes, Grandfather," answered the little girl sitting next to him, her small arms wrapped around his legs. "Besides Moon Wolf, Miss Alice was a woman of great courage. But Grandfather, how can she be a Blackfeet legend when she wasn't even Indian?"

The old man raised his chin, his eyes flickering

with an emotion that was almost unreadable. At length, he uttered, "Oh, my granddaughter, but she was of our tribe. For you see, being Blackfeet is not simply a matter of color of skin or the place where one is born. Being Blackfeet, my child, is a condition of the heart. *Áa,* yes, a condition of the heart. Remember this. The white man's ways may come and go, but so long as you remember us, the true and moral ways of your people, you will always prosper.

"And now I have spoken."

The old man hung his head, the young child at his side taking his hand in her own small one.

She whispered, "I will remember, Grandfather. I will always remember...."

The End

Genny Cothern

GENNY COTHERN's great grandmother was Choctaw and she is also adopted Blackfeet.

"With these short stories, I hope to bring to mind the American Indian's concept of honor and what it meant to live as free men and free women. There are some things worth remembering."

Made in the USA
Middletown, DE
24 June 2024

56042129R00043